MAY   2008

BUG BOOKS

Dragonfly

Stephanie St. Pierre

Heinemann Library
Chicago, IL

Customer Service 888-454-2279
Visit our website at www.heinemannraintree.com

Design: Kimberly R. Miracle and Cavedweller Studio
Illustration: David Westerfield

Color Reproduction by Dot Gradations Ltd, UK
Printed and bound in China by South China Printing Company

12 11 10 09 08
10 9 8 7 6 5 4 3 2 1

New edition ISBNs: 978 1 4329 1238 3 (hardcover)
                      978 1 4329 1249 9 (paperback)

The Library of Congress has cataloged the first edition as follows:
Dragonfly / Stephanie St. Pierre.
        p. cm. - - (Bug books)
Includes bibliographical references.
ISBN 1-58810-171-1 (lib. bdg.)
1. Dragonflies- - Juvenile literature. [1. Dragonflies.] I. Title. II. Series.
        QL520 .S74 2001
        595.7'33- -dc21
                                      00-011429

Acknowledgments
The publishers would like to thank the following for permission to reproduce photographs:
© Animals Animals pp. 5 (Maria Zorn), **8** (Stephen Dalton), **15** (Robert Armstrong), **19** (Robert Lubeck), **21** (Lynn M. Stone), **22, 24, 26** (Joe McDonald), **28** (John Gerlach); © Bruce Coleman pp. **6** (Kim Taylor), **9** (Kim Taylor), **14** (Gary Meszaros); © Dwight Kuhn p. **17**; © Getty Images (Marie Dubrac/ANYONE) p. **29**; © Oxford Scientific Films pp. **11** (G. I. Bernard), **25**; © Peter Arnold pp. **10** (Hans Pfletschinger), **27** (Joan Cancalosi); © Photolibrary pp. **4** (John Yurka), **20** (Dr F. Ehrenstrom & L. Beyer); © Photo Researchers pp. **7** (Gary Meszaros), **12** (E. R. Degginger), **13** (FLY D. NYM), **16** (Stephen Dalton), **23** (Kenneth H. Thomas); © Science Photo Library (Gary Meszaros) p. **18**.

Cover photograph of a dragonfly on dewey grasses reproduced with permission of Photolibrary (Nancy Rotenberg).

Every effort has been made to contact copyright holders of any material reproduced in this book. Any omissions will be rectified in subsequent printings if notice is given to the publisher.

Contents

Some words are shown in bold, **like this**. You can find out what they mean by looking in the glossary.

What Are Dragonflies?

Dragonflies are **insects**. They have six legs and long thin bodies.

leg

eye

body

wing

Dragonflies have two pairs of wings.
They have two big eyes and two
small **antennae**.

Dragonflies have a mouth with sharp **jaws** for grabbing and eating other bugs.

Most dragonflies are as long as your finger. Their wings can be wider than your hand. They can be green, blue, or red.

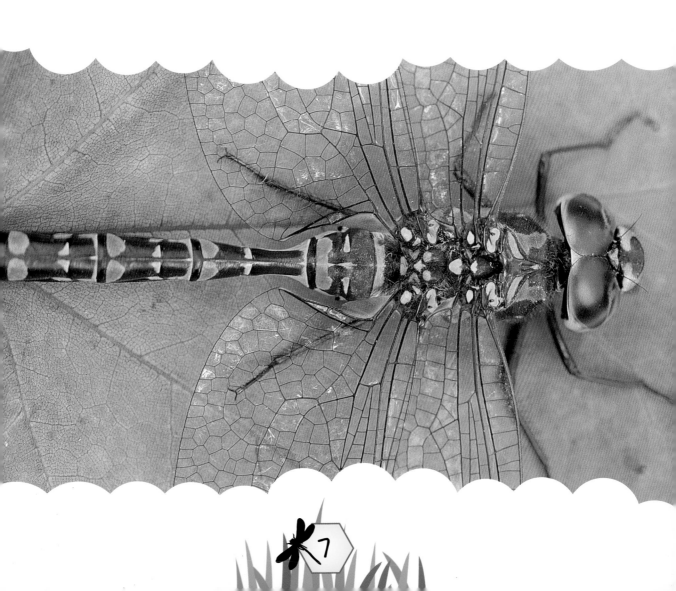

How Are Dragonflies Born?

Dragonflies lay eggs. Some lay their eggs in water. Other dragonflies use plants that grow near water. The eggs hatch after about four weeks.

The young dragonflies are called **nymphs**. They live in water. Nymphs do not have wings.

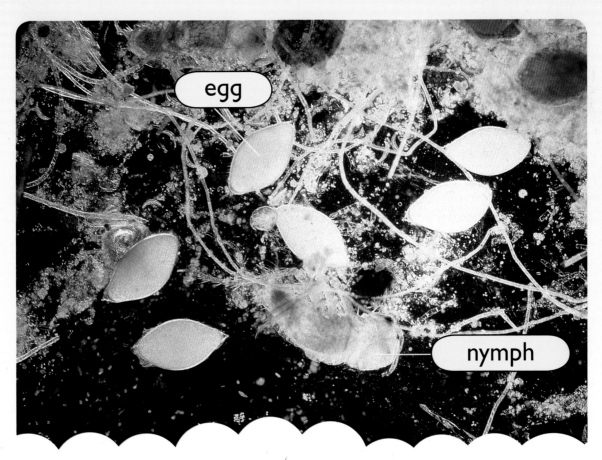

egg

nymph

How Do Dragonflies Grow?

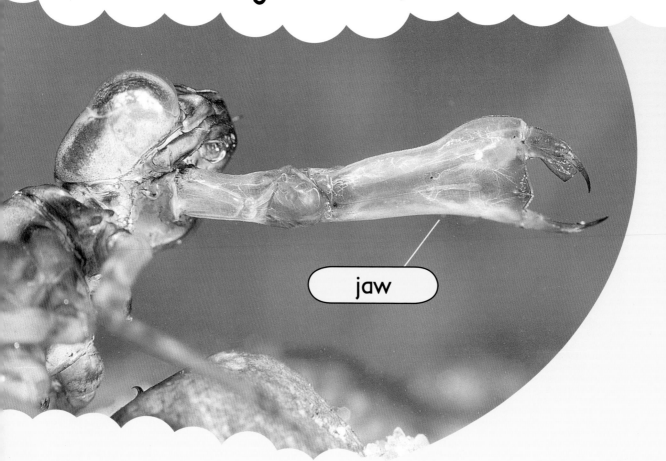

jaw

Dragonfly **nymphs** eat lots of mosquito **larvae**. The nymphs have a special **jaw** that shoots out from their mouth to grab **prey**.

old skin

As the nymphs grow, they shed their tight skin. This is called **molting**. They molt many times before they are fully grown.

11

At last the **nymph** is ready to change into an **adult** dragonfly. It climbs out of the water and onto a stem. It hangs on tight with its claws.

The nymph **molts**. It breaks out of its old skin for the last time. Now it has wings. It rests while its body gets dry and hard.

nymph

old skin

How Do Dragonflies Move?

Dragonfly **nymphs** cannot fly. They live in water. They move very fast by shooting water through their **gills**.

Adult dragonflies can fly very well. They can zigzag, turn, and even fly backwards.

What Do Dragonflies Eat?

nymph

Dragonfly **nymphs** are good hunters. They eat the **larvae** of other insects. As they grow bigger they eat **tadpoles**, small frogs, and even small fish.

Adult dragonflies hunt while they fly.
They have very good eyesight. This
helps them see other flying insects. They
catch them and eat them.

17

Which Animals Eat Dragonflies?

Birds and frogs like to eat dragonflies but they are hard to catch. They can fly very fast.

Birds and frogs catch dragonflies
when they are laying eggs or when
they are **molting**.

19

Where Do Dragonflies Live?

There are dragonflies in most parts of the world where there is water. Dragonfly **nymphs** live in water.

Adult dragonflies can fly a long way from water. They always fly back to lay their eggs.

How Long Do Dragonflies Live?

Most dragonfly **nymphs** live for a few years in water while they grow. Most **adult** dragonflies only live for a few months.

The most dangerous time for a dragonfly is when it changes from a nymph to an adult. It cannot fly away until its new wings and body are dry and hard.

What Do Dragonflies Do?

Dragonfly **nymphs** swim around water plants and hunt for food. Sometimes they lie at the bottom of a pond or lake.

Before they can fly, **adult** dragonflies must sit in the sun or shake and shiver to warm up the **muscles** in their wings.

How Are Dragonflies Special?

Dragonflies are very strong. They can lift things much heavier than themselves.

dragonfly

prey

There have been dragonflies for millions
of years. **Fossils** prove that they are
even older than dinosaurs. Some of those
dragonflies were as big as owls.

Thinking About Dragonflies

What must a dragonfly do before it is ready to fly? Why do dragonflies shiver?

Look out for dragonflies near ponds or lakes in the summer. What colors can you see?

Bug Map

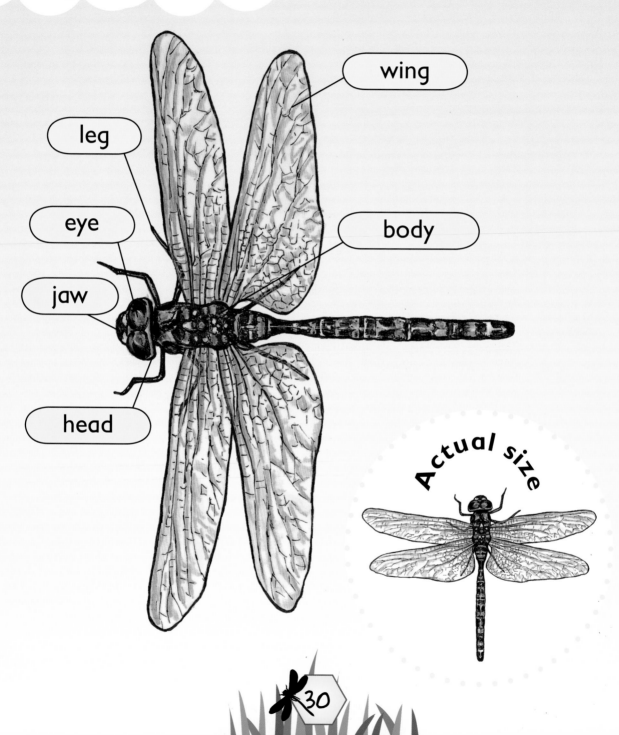

wing

leg

eye

body

jaw

head

Actual size

Glossary

adult grown-up

antenna (more than one = antennae) long thin tube that sticks out from the head of an insect. Antennae can be used to smell, feel, or hear.

fossil remains left in stone of an animal or plant that lived a long time ago

gill part of the body that takes air out of water so that animals can breathe in water

hatch break out of an egg

insect small animal with six legs and a body with three parts

jaw bony parts that make the shape of the mouth

larva (more than one = larvae) baby insect that hatches from an egg. It does not look like the adult insect.

molting time in an insect's life when it gets too big for its skin. The old skin drops off and a new skin is underneath.

muscle part of the body that helps it to move

nymph insect baby that has hatched from an egg

prey animal that is hunted for food

Index

More Books to Read

Allen, Judy. *Are You a Dragonfly? (Backyard Books)*. Boston, MA.: Kingfisher, 2004.

Coughlan, Cheryl. *Dragonflies*. Danbury, CT.: Capstone Press, 2000.